AF219123

FSC
www.fsc.org

MIX

Papier aus ver-
antwortungsvollen
Quellen
Paper from
responsible sources

FSC® C105338

Gudrun Rogge-Wiest

Sleepwalking

Dream narratives

Für meine family

and

for my friend Gudrun

Bibliografische Information der Deutschen Nationalbibliothek:
Die Deutsche Nationalbibliothek verzeichnet diese Publikation
in der Deutschen Nationalbibliografie; detaillierte bibliografische Daten sind im Internet über dnb.dnb.de abrufbar.

© 2023 Gudrun Rogge-Wiest
Herstellung und Verlag: BoD – Books on Demand, Norderstedt

ISBN: 978-3752894578

Table of Contents

Prologue

For more than a year, from Mai 2021 to August 2022 I have put into words as much as I could remember of my dreams. Right after waking up in the morning I sat myself down either in bed or in front of my desk writing with a pen on paper. Time and again I struggled with the apparently high resolution of the images dissolving while I was working on transcribing them. In the process some episodes or images took centre stage, others blurred or vanished completely. Although a dream catcher has been hanging over my bed since mother´s day of 2022, a present of my older daughter, the challenge has remained. What appeared to be prolific dream material at first, could be transcribed only incompletely.

Dreams are sometimes more eventful than real life, and they can draw attention to latent states of mind and correlations. As to method, I strove for a high degree of accuracy in the representation of scenes and experiences in order to enable my readers to relive them in their minds. In the process 'I', the subject of the dream world, becomes a first-person narrator distinct from the author. As reason does not interfere with the dreaming mind, dreams contain fault lines, occasionally take an absurd turn or enter the realms of the fantastic and supernatural. A character might initially seem to represent a certain person, but on closer inspection turns out to be someone else.

In its density, according to Sigmund Freud the result of concentration and displacement, the manifest dream content is comparable to the figurative language of literary texts.[1] Thus, transcribing my dreams, a collection of short prose texts with an anecdotal character has come into being.

It might be confusing that the first-person narrator can be a middle-aged woman in one dream and a youth in another. I considered arranging the dreams according to the age of the narrator. However, this would have meant giving up the randomness of theme which the chronological sequence reflects.

With the pioneer of psychoanalysis I share the fear of embarrassing oneself by giving the public an insight into the workings of my soul, and I find solace in the way he deals with this situation. In his own words in my translation:

> *It is understandable that one flinches from giving away material of such intimacy from one's emotional life. Doing so leaves one unable to protect oneself against misinterpretation by strangers. But one has to override these doubts.*[2]

---

[1] e.g. https://literaturkritik.de/id/15167. The essay is a short version of Joachim Pfeiffer's contribution 'Sigmund Freud (1856-1939)' in: Matias Martinez / Michael Scheffel (Hg.): *Klassiker der modernen Literaturtheorie*. Von Sigmund Freud bis Judith Butler. Verlag C. H. Beck, München 2010. S. 11-32.

[2] Sigmund Freud, *Die Traumdeutung* (1900), *Sigmund Freud Studienausgabe Band II,* Frankfurt am Main, 1972, 125.

In contrast to Freud, it is not my aim to analyse the dreams and to reconstruct the latent dream content.

Of course, the dream content is based on my experiences. Sometimes the material has been dug up from the remoter past, from youth or young adulthood. Many areas of life are covered and occasionally there are allusions to current issues.

My reservations with regard to publishing these dream narratives are not so much due to their content, as there is no one-to-one correspondence with real happenings. They are more like a fictional representation in that they refer indirectly to experiences I have had and often deal with them in fantasy plots and with character constellations rearranged.

However, I have been thinking long and hard about the characters´ names. After all, they represent real people I am close to: family members, friends and colleagues. So I cannot just use the usual disclaimer *All characters appearing in this work are fictitious. Any resemblance to real persons, living or dead, is purely coincidental*.[3] However, most people are unrecognizable as they do not appear as round characters in the dreams. They are often just by-standers or feature a very limited number of traits or behaviours. Still, some dreams do characterize actually existing relationships from the point of view of my dreaming self.

---

[3] e.g. in: http://en.wikipedia.org/wiki/All_persons_fictitious_disclaimer

To protect people´s privacy, I have decided to use letters instead of inventing names. Thus, I hope to be able to cover the tracks sufficiently without deleting the correspondences completely.

List of main characters

A	older brother
C	younger daughter
F	a boy-friend when I was a student
H	husband
J	older daughter
W	younger brother

May to August 2021

During the final minutes the participants of a workshop, me among them, are assigned to write a comment on an A4 sheet of paper. It is pinned to the wall in one corner of the big room, a school hall perhaps. Now, standing in front of it, I wonder what to write doubting if I have the right to judge. Besides, there are some things I don't want the other participants to know. So what could I write? The queue of people waiting behind me becomes longer and longer. Their perceived impatience weighs on me. Although I am usually slow under pressure, I am rescued by a brainwave. Why don't I just write down a question?

When I manage to carry out my task without blundering or being disturbed, I am immensely relieved and feel so self-confident that I spend some more time wondering if I should sign my work. And though evaluations are usually handed in anonymously, I decide to just add my initials: *Rw*. Everyone will recognize them. Once more I read through what I have written, and yes, it'll do.

Socialising

I am in the company of a colleague, a woman of approximately the same age. We are part of a mixed group of people on our way back from a trip and heading for a small train station somewhere in the country. It is the dead end of a single track with the train ready to board. The carriages are from an earlier age. They are earth-coloured and angular with an overhanging convex sheet metal roof.

Although we have twenty minutes to kill my companion urges us to get on it right away, because it has only two carriages. We sit down on seats in the corridor, but it is so narrow that leaning a little forward my forehead immediately touches the acrylic glass of the compartment opposite. It will be impossible for people to walk past us.

Now I am sitting in a large compartment around a table with a few elderly people. My place is at its head. On the table are two cakes both with chocolate icing. As one of them has already been cut into, I can see the thick layers of chocolate butter cream surrounded by crumbly black pastry. In anticipation I sense a spoonful of it melting on my tongue, smooth and cool with the bitter-sweet chocolaty taste of cocoa spreading across my taste buds. But it is not time to indulge in this, yet.

Meanwhile, I have taken a seat on one side of the table. To my right is an elderly man whom I have quite recently started seeing. He tells me about his late first wife, and I picture her as a very beautiful young woman. So I shrink back in dismay, when he shows me a photo of her with a wrinkled face and silver-grey hair so thin that the skin shines through. She looks ill and unhappy.

He quickly produces another photo on which her face is younger. Her hair is white and so bushy and curly that I wonder if it was reddish in her youth. He wants to remember his wife as she was as a young woman, he says. He must have noticed my reaction and tries to put me at ease again. But the affection I felt for him earlier is gone, and I wonder why I took to him and consented to seeing him.

Back at the head of the table, I notice that the chocolate cream cake has disappeared. There are only crumbs left. The second cake has been cut into, too. However, it does not have any cream inside, and plain sponge cake doesn´t tempt me much. So I find it easy to abstain. Besides, we are going to arrive at our destination, presently.

Hedge hopper   August 20

I stand at one of the windows of my parents´ house. It was built by my grandfather in 1938. My gaze wanders over the familiar features of the Brigach valley, which is bordered by a dark forest on the surrounding hills. It is summer. The sky, a cloudless, blue canopy, stretches to the horizon. Suddenly, the ear-splitting bang of an explosion makes the walls and the floor vibrate. The shock wave is passing through my body when the giant airplane, which has flown over our house, appears right in front of the window sinking before my very eyes. I can see every detail of its enormous wings and fuselage. It's bound to crash into the next row of houses. A ball of fire and wreckage is going to tear and burn down everything in its vicinity. It's all over.

But the plane just gains enough height to rise above the roof tops. It goes on flying at low altitude, so that for a short while I expect it to make an emergency landing in the Brigach valley, but it withdraws fast, the noise subsiding until all is silent. My house, my neighbourhood, my world, have remained unscathed this time.

Swimming

I am swimming in a quarry pond heading for the other shore which seems to be in convenient reach. The water is pleasantly balmy. I sense it lapping against my naked body and tugging gently in the opposite direction. I feel good, light and happy.

Inaugural meeting August 25

After a break of some years I have been elected town councillor again. It is the night of the inaugural meeting, and the big hall is crowded. But instead of the ceremony I expected, we have to vote on some issue right away without being briefed any further. I turn to some of my colleagues in a final effort to get the necessary information, but in vain. As I have resolved to prepare myself thoroughly, this makes me feel deeply embarrassed. Thus left in limbo I am unable to raise my hand, not even with those who abstain, all the time hoping that my confusion won´t be noticed.

A workshop August 28

During a workshop, in which F participates among others, we have to prepare a recital of a poem or some other suitable text. During the rehearsal, however, I am informed that I am disqualified. I am dejected and strongly disappointed. The reasons given remain incomprehensible to me and are not explained any further, which makes me feel mutinous, because I am still confident that my text is special and worth reading out in front of an audience.

September to December 2021

A lakeside walk   September 21

My ten-year-old daughter C and I are on the little
ferry boat that crosses one of the arms of Lake Constance. It docks at the pleasure port of Überlingen,
and we disembark. We walk along the lakeside heading for Meersburg. The road is closed to traffic and at
its end there is an opening onto a footpath leading
gently uphill. We follow it until we have reached an
altitude of about fifty metres above the surface of the
lake. From here, the path is level, and we walk on
skirting the bellies of the vineyards. The vines are full
of grapes, in some rows they are green, in others almost black with the berries bulging with juice. Unable
to resist I pick one of them, put it into my mouth and
let it burst between my tongue and my palate. With
the fruity sweetness of the juice I taste the lightness
and happiness of this late summer´s day, and simultaneously drink in the view in front of us of the mountain ranges across the lake on the Swiss side.

   When, on an impulse, I turn around, however, I am
horrified at the sight of a giant industrial plant tower-
ing between the hills behind the crescent of the north-
ern shore. From its tall chimneys billowing black
smoke rises into the reddish sky.

Force of gravity

I am somewhere around the house on a hillside by Lake Constance where I lived as a student and enjoy the view across Mainau Island, the lake and the hills on the opposite shore. I wear my lab coat open at the front. Now I button it up bottom up.

I look forward to going for a run. My route leads through the forest on the nearby ridge with its dense and cool vaults of foliage. Time passes, and I really want to go, but something indefinite keeps me back. I wonder what it might be. Why can´t I just get moving when I am all motivated?

The drink   November 4

It is during a reception. The hall is packed. I promise H to fetch him a glass of fruity white wine and head for the long table at its upper end next to the entrance. A buffet is spread on a white paper cloth with plates and glasses on one side. There, two people are taking orders for drinks. When it´s my turn, I am poured a shot. Balancing the shot glass I turn round and thread my way back through the other guests. All the time I have a sense of foreboding. What will happen when I am going to hand him the wrong drink.

Climbing a cliff

We climb an almost perpendicular cliff in the mountains in single file with our feet finding a foothold on steps that seem to have been carved into it by nature. So far I have been up to the task, all strength and agility. H, who is the lead climber, instructs the eleven to twelve year-old C behind him where to put her hands and feet. We have almost made it to the top. There are only two to three metres left. Below us a chasm studded with jaggy rock formations yawns. I shudder and firmly repress the idea of anything causing us to lose our grip when I overhear H warning C about a loose stepping stone, which is difficult to bypass. We have to try hard to shift our weight to be able to tread on it only lightly, so that it won´t yield to the pressure. The stability of the rocks piled onto it depends on it not breaking out. My insides contract with fear. I feel queasy. While glad that the stone carries C´s weight, if only just, I realize how likely it is that it´ll give under mine.

On skis

A brown, barren autumn landscape surrounds me. I stand on skis on a paved, narrow road on the edge of a plateau. From there the road drops gently. I scrape and jerk along. In front of me to the left the slope is steeper and surprisingly, it is covered with so much snow that the grass peeks through only in a few places. I slide down heading for a chapel located on a terrace. It is cream coloured with purple sand stone ledges. From there the first houses of a village in the valley below come into view, somehow familiar and strange at the same time. Where am I? I ask myself as I push off to glide further downhill, because it´s so easy, wondering what is going to await me.

The Bassoon   December 15

I visit G. They have an open-plan living room with a gallery in front of the bedrooms on the first floor. W is with me. We are on one side of the gallery and see a bassoon but without its mouthpiece standing on the opposite side. W says it is a bass flute. We wonder where the missing mouthpiece might be. At this moment the instrument tips over the railing and falls down. I see it in my mind´s eye gone to splinters, yet there is no crash. It is lying on the tiled ground floor, miraculously unharmed.

Meeting a friend

Now, we sit at a table in the outdoor area of a café on a busy road. G´s daughter is standing behind her. They talk about their plans. When they go on to devise a schedule for a number of outings, I begin to feel excluded, but G has already changed the subject. Now we are discussing when and where to meet again.

Preparations for a war   December 20

A war is looming. Everyone is involved in the preparations. It is my mission to creep into a car that is covered with aluminium foil for camouflage. A guardsman holds me back explaining that this is impossible because it means tearing the seamless wrapping, but I insist and worm my way through the driver´s door and over the clutch across to the passenger seat. Instead of the door there is a concrete wall with a niche carved out at eye-level. I reach in and find nuts, hazel nuts, bound together with a congealed substance like chocolate.

When I crawl back, my knickers tear. In fact they are the new white ones that got snagged in the laundry. Nothing to be done but to bin them, I conclude.

Chaos December 22

I try to get my bearings in a large room crammed with furniture where people are lounging in arm chairs and glass shards are lying on the floor. It is supposed to be my fault and I feel guilty.

There is a noise like hail pattering on a metal sheet roof. A multitude of little green balls is scuttling over a baking tray and caught by its raised edge. They turn out to be peas.

There's a rustling and scraping from inside a crate. A huge colourful insect shaped like a stag beetle lifts the lid. It feels creepy, the more because I didn't expect the insect to be able to do this by itself.

Dark clouds

On a walking tour I pass through a village somewhere in the uplands. I have already left the centre with the church as its landmark behind me and walk along the narrow main road flanked by two-storey houses, former farm houses with living space on one side and a barn on the other. Behind the village the road turns uphill. It is a mellow, sunny day. The shrubs at the wayside are studded with the berries of late summer. Behind them stretch lean uneven meadows with here and there a solitary big old fruit tree. Warm yellowish-orange to reddish hues compete with the green of mid-summer.

I proceed uphill and stop on a saddle overlooking the valley and the surrounding hills. Immediately, the thick black canopy of clouds hanging over its opposite end and enveloping the hills beyond catches my eye. A thunder storm is looming. I decide to interrupt my tour and to seek shelter in the village.

A group of walkers approaches. Absorbed in their conversation they pass by without acknowledging me and take the path leading downhill into the valley. Haven´t they seen the clouds, yet? I wonder. The coming storm will be at least extremely disagreeable if not dangerous. Shall I warn them?

The first gentle rain drops dissolve on my skin, and I turn back. Maybe there is a nice café in the village centre. I doubt that there will be a free table though as earlier, the streets around the square were quite busy.

Staff outing   December 23

It is our annual staff outing. As usual, we go for a long walk first. Now, the path leads gently downhill along a cone-shaped mountain covered only by low vegetation. At the bottom it runs along a brook that ultimately reaches the beach and finally the sea.

We walk in a long file that has split up into smaller groups and sometimes pairs. I am with Ha. The sun shines with such an intensity that we suffer from the heat of this late summer day. The shrubs lining the path and dotting the meadows are not high enough to cast any shade.

On the opposite side of the brook is a similar cliff. Behind it a mountain range stretches along the horizon. A hiker, who has climbed down the cliff, approaches and stops to talk to us. He points into the distance at one of the peaks where a building is visible, shimmering in the sun and flashing back its rays. A glass palace? A palace made of ice? A transparent cuboid sits in an oblique angle on an equally transparent cube as its foundation.

'This is a popular destination for teachers,' he says. The building seems far away and alien and we struggle to whip up some enthusiasm. We promise to make a mental note.

A chemistry lesson

The setting is a science laboratory at a school. I am supposed to give my lesson in the same room as my colleague Mi. Each of us teaches a group of senior students. With her resonant voice in the background I find it hard to focus, and I doubt that my students can follow my explanations.

Now, our experiments are ready for analysis. We examine and compare the plants we have grown. In order to help the students with their assignments, I point out the significant differences and realize that it is not easy to see them.

In the meantime silence has fallen. I look around and realize that only a few people are left in the room. Mi and her class have disappeared and some of my own students are missing, too. How could this escape me? I am suffused with shame. One student explains that they are heading to the nearby castle ruin. I am relieved that Mi has taken this liberty. In future, given a similar situation, this will be an option for me, too.

At the pool December 24

I am standing at the edge of a pool with two female colleagues. Sa tells me that she doesn´t mind me joining her. While we climb one after the other down the ladder and plunge into the water, however, she adds something along the lines of:

'Though I don´t have anything against you coming along, plainly speaking, I need some space, above all when I gaze at the mirror image of the big glass cupola on the huge building nearby. Imagine, the pattern of letters on its surface is perfectly reconstructed in the water.'

She takes the lead. I swim after her towards the end of the lane grateful for her kindness and also curious, looking forward to the experience. It is like starting on an adventure.

From the other end of the lane I notice the spotlessly dark blue canopy of the sky above. Only far in the distance does it lighten and gradually turn bright yellow. On the horizon, where it has merged with the darker red rising from the surface of the earth, it has turned a fiery orange. My gaze wanders to the building with the cupola now lit from within and then to the image below the surface of the water. However, I can only see a small segment of the original with a letter here and there. I feel slightly disappointed. Why on earth are these letters so important to her? I wonder. Not until later do I realize that it might have helped to climb onto the edge of the pool.

The hotel room

On a walking tour H and I reach a saddle with a hotel. From there our route continues downhill, first gently then more steeply. H, however, turns left and walks to the hotel. Somewhat surprised I follow him into the restaurant to the bar where he is talking to someone. When I join him he says that before resuming our walk, he has to pack his things, go to the toilet.

'Me too,' I reply, and go upstairs to my room, which, however, I am unable to find. The door I have opened leads into H´s room. To my surprise it is a spacious suite, a bit crammed though by furniture, which gives it a labyrinthine character. The door to the bathroom is locked, but around the corner there is a toilet bowl. I sit down and start urinating. Listening to the rushing stream, I enjoy the relief and relax, when I hear the door to the suite open. Two men, one of them H, approach talking to each other. They come ever closer. Glad that I am done I wipe myself hastily and just about manage to pull up my trousers. While I squeeze past the men on my way to the door, I stammer something to dispel the suspicion of sneaking in. He shouldn´t mind, though. After all, he is my husband.

Back in the corridor I am astonished to see Bi. She is the wife of Be, H´s companion in the suite. And what an extravagantly luxurious apartment it is, I think. Bi and Be, who are friends of ours, very likely share my opinion, and Be, in particular, will be quietly amused.

Bi starts haranguing on men in the manner of a rap. She moves to the rhythm and occasionally hits the wall with the ball of her hand. I would like to join in, but am unable to think of anything she hasn´t already brought up. Neither can I sway and dance to her rhythm. So I lurch and totter helplessly in the corridor feeling stiff, clumsy and intellectually inferior.

Balcony scene

I am standing under a balcony when I sense drops of liquid hitting the crown of my head. I look up and see someone leaning over the railing. My tongue catches one of the drops. It tastes like a cheap alcoholic drink pepped up with artificial fruity flavours - disgusting. Afraid that the drops will soil my hair I retreat from the area of the balcony.

Purgatory

December 29

In the staff room. A trainee teacher asks me for a quiz for English learners at a certain stage of year 7 or 8. She shows me what is suggested in the text book.

'I don´t have anything here at the moment,' I say, which is true. Besides, I don´t have the time for a longer search. I feel sorry, because I like to help out. On the other hand my refusal has liberated me from the pressure of providing something.

Not much later I enter the trainee teacher´s class room, in order to announce something. It only takes a few words to make them listen, which makes me happy. While I am speaking, pupils in the back row exchange remarks.

'Her name is Gudrun,' I hear.

The news spreads fast and finally several pupils in the back call 'Hello Gudrun'. I say a few words to restore order, but others have joined the hunt.

'She is in love with Mr P. Hello Mrs P,' they chant.

The missing piece

It is in St. Martin´s church. I am sitting among my colleagues to the left of the aisle at the front opposite the chancel. We are called by our names. One after the other, my colleagues get up with their musical instruments and walk to the chairs set up for the orchestra in the space between the chancel, the pews and the altar steps. When I hear my name I realize with a touch of sadness that I won´t be able to play the oboe because I haven´t got any workable double reeds. Why on earth haven´t I remembered to sort this out in time? Ashamed of myself, I decide to remain sitting in the pew.

Before court   December 30

I am sitting in a room on the first floor of a house. With a sense of foreboding I wait to be called down and submit to a hearing about a false statement I have made. Something was wrong with a document in a folder. It turned out to be a fake. Asked who could have committed the offence, I put forward another person's name although I knew the real culprit. My false testimony was discovered and now a court is deliberating on my case. I deeply regret my behaviour. Why I acted like this is a mystery to me. I did not have any sympathy for, not to speak of emotional attachment to the offender. Besides, it runs contrary to my natural disposition to tell an untruth. Expecting a severe judgment and in the wake of it social exclusion, I feel much oppressed.

Now, I hear them call my name from downstairs. The judges, M and G, are much kinder than expected. By their grace I am rehabilitated and allowed to return to the upper part of the house. My mood lifts. I leave the room relieved that everything went so well. Instead of the wooden staircase I descended earlier, however, I find myself mounting a ladder, a rope ladder but in the form of a net. Whenever I put my foot on the next rung, it yields and sways to and fro. I have to keep the edges apart with my hands to prevent it from rolling up into a spiral. It takes a tremendous effort, but I make headway feeling optimistic. After some time, however, I start to wonder where the ladder leads, and it occurs to me that there might not be an exit from it to the first or any of the other floors of the house, at all.

The inheritance

M is talking to his oldest son. In a voice somewhere between aggrieved and angry he lists the items of his inheritance. He concludes by adding that without exception they are assets. If he wanted to spend money on a larger scale he would have to raise a mortgage on them.

Disaster

Human bodies are tumbling down the staircase and remain lying before me at the foot of the stairs bleeding and with severe injuries. I tell myself that I haven't done anything to bring this about. Nevertheless, it is my duty to help. Yet, taking in the number of the injured and the degree of their injuries I am paralysed, unable to decide what would be the best and right thing to do and what to do first. So caught between the options, I wake up feeling utterly helpless.

Confused   December 31

After the lesson I enter the staff room and walk to my desk, which I recognize from its position in relation to the other rows of tables and the windows. I have also deposited lesson material and my briefcase, there. Suddenly, I realize, that I sit in the wrong place, one row further to the back and more in the middle. What´ll my colleagues think? I wonder, painfully embarrassed. I glimpse Sa in the row behind me. Hoping that she won´t notice I grab as many of my things as possible and carry them to my desk.

The demonstration

It is almost the beginning of the next lesson. I pick up my material and step into the hall. On turning right I note a demonstration approaching from the left led by our shop steward. He is carrying a banner displaying a demand or a slogan. Still, I am unable to deduce what they demonstrate for or against, and I wonder about the consequences for the lessons. Are the participants going to interrupt them and even tell the classes to join their procession?

January to April 2022

Delayed January 1

A man is cross-examined on his right-wing extremist views before a court in Karlsruhe. Apart from me an older man looking like Bernie Sanders is listening. He says he is aware of my merits, and that he is going to escort me to the station. I am nervous because my train departs, soon, but the frame of my bike is bent. I have to straighten it out first.

Suddenly it´s not a bike anymore, but my parents´ buggy from the 1960s with its heavy metal frame. I unfold it, sit astride it and push off with my feet. Meanwhile, the man has walked on. When I catch up he says with his voice tinged with disappointment that my train departs in two minutes and that I´ll miss it. This would be a disaster. I would be late for the two double lessons in English and Science I always have on Monday afternoons. I think about assignments for my English class, which I could e-mail to the vice head teacher´s office. The science class would have to be cancelled.

Now, the older man is standing in a group of people absorbed in a conversation. He ignores me, so I ask a passer-by for directions to the train station. Surprisingly, it is right here, a grey, cubic building with open-work concrete walls.

'If you hurry, you will catch your train,' she says.

I run off.

Spring   January 6

It is winter. After a phase with abundant snow, temperatures have risen during the day, but the melt water still freezes again at night. I drive my car on a parking covered by ice. As it is empty, I head for the rear and park in a right angle to the entrance lane.

The air feels like early spring, still cold, but lacking the bite of winter. Between the dark clouds patches of sky glow yellow. I am invited to a party. A long beer table nearby is laden with a cornucopia of food. There are assorted dishes and salads with bowls of fruit and baskets of bread in between.

At the edge of the parking I notice a stream gurgling through the meadow into the valley. Behind it, children are playing football. Suddenly the ball lands with a splash on the surface of the water and is carried away by the current. One of the football players, a girl, heads for the stream. As I expect the ball to gain speed and want to prevent it from getting lost, I run after it, too, overtake it, then turn around and reach for it. However, it eludes my grasp and is carried further downwards by the water. It looks bigger and lighter than a football, now, not unlike a beach ball, but almost white and covered with grey octagons. I wonder what kind of game it is used for.

Still in pursuit of the ball, I jump into the stream and proceed supernaturally nimbly and light-footed without spraining my ankle or slipping on one of the rocks. Further downstream someone is standing by the bank. He could easily pick up the ball when it floats past him, but I don´t stop chasing it, skip one last time and catch it. Proudly and happily I walk towards the man who hasn´t budged in the meantime. It is Mr S, a retired senior colleague.

Now I am sitting next to Mr S on a bench in a wooden shelter without walls, just a gabled roof above a wooden table to which two wooden benches are fastened. He offers me a roll of ham by impaling it on a fork and raising it to my mouth. According to him the recipe is worth knowing if one wants to have access to the ranks of the cultured.

Anxious not to be considered backward I take a bite. With his eyes focused on me I cannot but indicate that it is delicious though contrary to my expectations the filling has turned out to be a gherkin instead of melon cubes. He nods his approval.

'Ham rolls are just an example of the many delicious recipes I know,' he says.

I remember the buffet by the parking. It seemed to me sumptuous, close to wastefulness. By contrast, the ham roll is spartan, not more than a starter. I pine for some bread or a bread roll to go with it in order to offset its predominantly salty taste.

Falling apart

I sit among pupils of my senior English class discussing an assignment with them. After grasping the basics, they are ready to embark on the really interesting work. However, their motivation flags. They get restless and start to slink away. The group literally falls apart till no-one besides myself is left. I am downcast, at first, but then I notice that it´s almost 5 past 10. So time is up, anyway. I gather my things and head for my next class.

When I open the classroom door, I see another teacher greeting her class. The students stand to show their respect. This doesn´t happen in my classes, I think. How does she do this? In the next classroom the lesson has already started. I close the door quietly. I have lost my bearings with no clue whatsoever where my class could be.

Lost and found January 16

I drive a car with one of my daughters riding shotgun. We have just made a U-turn and are on our way back to the station, because we lost a recharger and my earbuds from Ireland with the shamrock stickers. To dispel a twinge of impatience I tell myself that it is not far. We turn left, cross the bridge to the other side of the railway, turn right and go straight on along the rails to the station. On entering the premises we immediately see the lost white objects hanging on a banister and gladly retrieve them.

Cross-country skiing

J and I set out to do some cross-country skiing on a flat-topped hill somewhere in the Black Forest. Due to a shortage of snow there are large gaps in the track, and we struggle to get ahead. After a while I stop and turn around to check for J, who catches up with me presently. When we look down the adjacent slope, we see an uninterrupted blanket of snow in the valley. We decide to put off our skis and walk downhill across the meadow that separates us from it. In fact there is snow in abundance, down there. In the sky, however, dark, deep-hanging clouds have gathered making the surroundings appear gloomy. Nevertheless, we put on our skis again and off we go.

In a mountain hut

Snacks are spread out on a table in a mountain hut. I am in the company of some of my colleagues. They are talking about a recent week-long trip that we have made together. A colleague remembers in indignant tones that one of us never joined in, when we were sitting together in the evenings. He gazes at me, but I reject the charge. When the others support me, I am surprised and glad.

Now, preparing to leave, we collect and pack things that are lying around. Suddenly the room resembles the staff room for a short while, then we are back in the mountain hut.

Before leaving we stretch out on our bunk beds to rest. I am lying on my back next to U, so close to him that our cheeks touch from time to time. Can this be wholly by accident? I do not feel attracted to him, though. Meanwhile his four to five year-old son has planted himself on a ledge on my other side. I wonder why we are still here instead of on our way home.

In India   January 18

I am in a motel room on the ground level. F and his parents are in the next room. We get ready for a coming journey by plane. The area in front of our rooms is a parking covered with red sand. Like a giant stove it gives off the heat it collected by refracting 24/7 the rays of the bright yellow sun ball hovering in the grey sky.

Port manoeuver

I stand on the deck of a ship next to the helmsman who is wearing a grizzled full beard and a navy blue cap. The cool wind brushes my face and tugs at my clothes. He looks straight ahead with his eyes narrowed to a slit while he is navigating the ship through the entrance of the port.

A walk in the mountains   January 30

During a family holiday in the mountains we walk uphill from our guest house to a plateau-shaped saddle. Looking around I am surprised to see the mountaintop close by, a clay-coloured almost completely barren cupola with boulders peeking out of the soil on its slopes. A steep path winds upwards through them with here and there stairs as if hewn into the rock. This looks easy, I think and say to H:

'I´d like to go up there. It won´t take long.'

Now I see people walking around at the top and there is even a cableway. A cabin is just entering its upper terminus, a hole in a concrete cube. I head for the rim of the plateau. There, I take in the breath-taking view of the deep valleys and the surrounding mountains. Then, looking down I flinch. The tips of my shoes are already over the edge of the precipice. Sobered by my carelessness I withdraw and just walk around the platform keeping well away from it. My gaze wanders over the mountain landscape and my mood lifts. Soon I am as enraptured as before.

Trying to communicate

H and I have just set out on a boat trip around the famous waterways of Mosel[4]. Our vessel is not a typical boat. It looks more like a horse-drawn carriage. I start to tell him about my recent encounter with two women. One of them is a lesbian, the other does not want to have sex any more. Their experiences have led me to crucial insights I would like to share with him. I hope that I can make him see through my lens, but hampered by a sense of inadequacy I struggle to put my thoughts into words. The harder I try the more indefinite the building I want to erect in front of his eyes seems to be. Besides, anxiety has snuck in. Does he suspect I am talking about my own sexual orientation, about my own emotions? I feel unsettled and digress citing an article about the disagreeable experiences of a lesbian couple who had to face ignorance and hostility from one of the partners´ parents.

---

[4] A fictional town.

Before the return journey

It´s the end of our family holiday on the day before the journey back home. We have just returned from a day trip, and it´s time to start packing our things. Some of them are spread around the big living room, and I am unsure where to begin. Anyway, we have to prepare dinner, first. H checks the pantry for vegetables. He passes me some courgettes and asks me to stew them. I start to dice them feeling honoured by his request.

A room with a view

Looking out of the window of my parents´ living room I am surprised to see the peaks of mountains covered in snow. Though I know this to be impossible, the sight lifts my mood. I point it out to the people in the room convinced by now that it is not an illusion. After all, clouds would have long changed their shape. The mountains, however, are still there, not far away, their solidity undeniable.

At the doctor´s February 1

After a long break I have an appointment with my GP. They take blood and measure my shoulder width. When the doctor shows me the results of the blood tests, they turn out to be a list of figures that don´t make any sense. When asked how I am, I give an account of my experience at the university hospital where the examinations did not lead to a definite diagnosis.

At once there are more people in the surgery. Nevertheless, I continue my report. The new people, both men and women, seem to be doctors, but they are having their own conversation. No-one is listening to me, any more. Finally I ask an elderly woman to write a prescription. She starts to write, and I hope that I´ll get the right medication.

A family party

It is at a big family party. People are spread around a spacious flat. They are sitting or standing in small groups. A breakfast buffet has been laid out on a long table. I have just arrived and amble from room to room to get an overview of the situation. Finally I let my gaze wander over the dishes on the table and breathe in their aroma.

As I feel grubby in my clothes, I walk to a wardrobe to select something nice to wear. In fact, there are some decent dresses, for example the light-green sleeveless one with the oblique neckline. Yet, none seems to be suitable for the occasion.

I move on to a table nearby, where O is about to slice a loaf of bread. When I sit down there, he gets up and leaves.

Doubts

I am on a cycle tour in the Black Forest in the company of a man. I lead the way. Rolling downhill on a steep, narrow road that crosses a brook in the valley and then runs up the opposite slope my front wheel drags. Am I going to have a flat tyre? I stop and check the pressure by shifting my weight onto it. Some air has been lost, but not enough to explain why it takes so much strength to move forward.

Looking around I am suddenly riddled with doubts though I have been so sure. Have we lost our way?

Two presents

In the entrance hall of a house or flat there is a parcel, which I unpack in the presence of a couple. It contains two presents. One of them is wrapped in fancy paper, the other wrap is crumpled and torn in places. Obviously, it has been used before.

The former contains a poster. The latter likewise yields a poster, exactly the same as the first. My friends are in raptures about the beautiful presents.

'So generous,' the woman remarks with a tinge of envy in her voice.

The solution   February 3

I am a pupil sitting in a classroom. We get an assignment based on the sketch of a convex disc. It is pierced at a sharp angle by an arrow and reminds me of a brooch. Confident of having found the solution despite the short time, I offer to present it to the class. When I stand in front of my classmates, however, I realize that I have misunderstood the instructions. We should have solved a different, text-based problem. So I begin to improvise.

Giving birth

On returning home I pass by people in the narrow dark entrance hall deep in conversation. I recognize my landlords and overhear them talking about my mother. She has given birth to a child on this door step, they say.

A safe space

It is in a café at the beach of a seaside resort. C and I are having coffee and a piece of cake on the terrace. After some time we withdraw to spend the night in the shelter provided by the crescent-shaped far side of a cliff.

I have just woken up and look for a pen and a sheet of paper to note down my dream. Now, I hear the rhythmic dark booming of the surge on the other side of the cliff. I lie awake anxiously awaiting each blow. My throat contracts painfully with fear. Are we going to be safe here?

A sense of foreboding   February 4

I am one in a circle made up of a few men. While listening to their elaborations, on how to insulate a house I own or which I am interested in buying, I realize that one of them is ill. He looks so haggard that I am afraid he'll die, soon, and I sense the dark painful emptiness he'll leave when he is gone.

When we meet a short time later, he is much better. His health has improved unexpectedly, and I am glad.

A lesson with a consultant
February 16

I teach English in year 8 or 9. The class consists almost exclusively of girls. They are good-natured and simultaneously interested and motivated. Now, they are focused on their assignment.

G is sitting among the pupils in the role of a consultant. Five minutes before the bell rings concentration starts to flag. I remember that I ought to give them their homework. Leafing through the text book, an exercise based on images catches my eye, but I haven't done it myself, yet. Besides, I realize that it is more important for the pupils to learn the new words that came up with today's new text. In the vocabulary section of my book, however, the relevant pages are missing. From the look of it they were torn out. Too bad. Meanwhile, my pupils have started to pack their school bags. Though doubting whether the message would reach them with all the noise, I raise my voice as much as I can to give them the page and number of the exercise.

On the whole I feel that the lesson went well though I am aware that I have made some unfortunate decisions towards the end. With students already jostling in for the next lesson, G urges me to find an empty room for our counselling interview. On stepping into the hallway, however, we are carried along with the tide of bodies rather than moving of our own free will until we are spat out through the entrance doors.

Now we are standing on a narrow path behind an ox cart. G suggests that we ask for a ride. However, we are stuck behind the cart unable to get past it to ask the driver's permission. Now the ox is taking a step forward. When he sets his hoof on the eroded slope, the sand gives. The ox's hind legs fold under his body and he slides on his backside downhill. We burst out laughing because it looks so funny. When I realize, however, that the ox is visibly humiliated, I feel pity. Ashamed of my behaviour I stop myself at once.[5]

---

[5] The scene with the ox cart must have been inspired by my reading of *Growing*, the second volume of Leonard Woolf's autobiography, which contains an account of a thirty-six hour journey by bullock cart during his time in Ceylon, today Sri Lanka. Leonard Woolf, *Growing*, An Autobiography of the Years 1904-1911, London, Harcourt, 1975, S. 23-30.

The white horse February 18

After mounting the hill on the other side of the valley from the town, I have just entered the forest. The leafy outer edge soon turns into an interior of dark spruces. I step onto the asphalt road, the lower bend of an *S* running diagonally along the slope to the top. A big, bony white horse materializes not far away from me and approaches at a walk. From closer up he looks very old. I have an urge to stop him, turn him around and lead him back to the horse farm on the other side of the hill. But am I strong enough? He seems so huge that he´ll just knock me over if I don´t step aside.

I am surprised that he really stops and stands still, when I grasp his bridle under the bit. His coat is thick with unusually long white and yellow hairs that have curled with sweat on his neck and shoulder. A girl, between five and seven years old, is sitting or rather hanging on his back. She is draped over the horse´s neck with her right cheek leaning against it and has wrapped her arms around his throat. Her face is veiled by her long, blond hair. I speak to her to attract her attention, but she does not respond. When I try to lift her and take her down, I realize that she is as good as attached to the horse.

Is she still alive? I wonder, struck with horror.

Just a dream   February 19

I walk around a city through streets lined by town houses in the style of late 19th century historicism. Though confident of knowing my way around this area, the adjoining modern brick houses seem unfamiliar. Have I overlooked the right turning? Luckily there seems to be an alley leading to the parallel street so that I won´t have to backtrack. It leads gently uphill between blocks of houses and is interspersed by occasional stairs. Two young adults, a man and a woman, a couple perhaps, are standing on one of the landings immersed in a heated conversation. He accuses her of something. The name *Robert* comes up. She switches to a purposely calm tone of voice to dispel his fears.

When I reach the parallel street, I join the many young people hanging around there like at a street festival. Somehow I find myself talking to a 20-year-old man with soft features. His name is Sebastien[6]. He tells me about his dream of travelling on a cargo ship around the world. He seems very young, vulnerable. I picture the freight ship putting out to sea, leaving its home port of Hamburg, perhaps, and momentarily I share in his exhilaration. Then, gradually, it is overlaid with a sense of foreboding that he won´t ever be able to make his dream come true.

There is J among the young people. She is in animated conversation with some of her former classmates and friends from the time before she left the

---

[6] He is a fictional character.

town. Evidently, they have made her feel welcome, their faces still beaming with joy about her being back. A young man with thick, wavy hair framing his round face catches my eye, but I don´t recognize him. Strangely, I don´t know anyone in this group. Did I interest myself so little in J´s life, then?

They are waving good bye, now, and scatter to meet again sometime later. It looks as if she were finally one of them in a way she had not been before she left. I am relieved to find her nervousness thus unfounded.

The scene has changed. I sit in a restaurant at a table in the far corner with my back against the wall. The young waiter who serves me rice and mixed vegetables on a plate turns out to be Sebastien. The meal is delicious. The vegetables are tasty and done, but not slushy. The rice is just as it is supposed to be. I chew thoroughly and let the aroma linger on the taste buds of my tongue and gums.

Later, I go into raptures about my lunch in a conversation with a woman on a narrow but busy alleyway.

'The best risotto I have ever had,' I claim. 'What an excellent cook they have with Sebastien.'

The woman gazes at me in amazement. Obviously, she does not share my view that Sebastien`s skills are extraordinary. J asks me whether I am in love with Sebastien. I examine my feelings thoroughly, but only find a motherly affection.

When he crosses my path again, I don´t even recognize him at first.

'Robert?' I ask. I notice that he is offended, but my gaffe is not the only reason for his dejection. Meanwhile he has come to the conclusion that he won't be able to realize his dream of a sailing trip around the world, ever. We are sitting side by side on the top step of a flight of stairs between the reddish facades of blocks of town houses. His head is resting on my shoulder, and I have put my arm around him willing to sustain his spirits, but doubtful whether I will be able to cheer him up.

An investigation   February 25

I am walking with a female friend along a corridor on the ground floor of a hotel, when two police officers emerge from the last room on the right, just before the door to the lobby. Evidently, they have searched it without finding anything. I am glad not to be in the focus of their investigation.

We follow them out into the street. They go on crossing it and entering the courtyard of one of the buildings where they stop to look at a sculpture. Intrigued, I watch them talking excitedly with each other as if surprised. After a while they turn away and go on to the next sculpture, a group of figures, and then to a third one that features chubby figurines on a high pedestal. They are carved out of a shining material like polished marble. I gather that the title of this work of art is *Blède* or *Bede* and that it has probably been stolen from an exhibition in Stoke on Trent.

Shopping for clothes · February 26

I stand in front of a revolving clothes-stand in a department store. I turn it slowly scanning the tops a bit listlessly and cluelessly. C approaches with assorted upscale tops draped over her arm, which she puts on display for me to choose from. I have collected some pairs of trousers, among them jeans, and a printed T-shirt. She laughs about the T-Shirt deeming it too casual.

'Hang it back up,' she directs.

Though I agree with her, the load on my arms is such that I am unable to lay down or return any item separately. Hoping that she doesn't suspect me of being reluctant to take advice I head for the changing booths.

A church service

I have just entered a church and stand at the back letting my gaze wander. The cone-shaped nave is spacious. The light falling through the long, colourful windows overlays the sobriety of the concrete walls and fills the room with a warm spiritual glow.

Rows of stairs are arranged in a crescent facing the altar. Many of them are empty. Two women are standing in front of the parishioners reading out aloud, surprisingly in English. Even more strangely, their text turns out to be a passage from a novel by Jane Austen which I have rediscovered for myself recently. [7] How is this supposed to be appropriate? I wonder, certain that not all the members of the audience will be able to make sense of the quote. Simultaneously, being in the vanguard with regard to my cultural interests makes me feel grimly satisfied, though not without a touch of self-irony.

At a café   March 3

I sit in front of my computer writing an e-mail to L confirming a date he has suggested. Then I walk between town houses along a street in a city. The young

---

[7] Around this time I reread Jane Austen's *Pride and Prejudice* before going to sleep to divert my attention from the war in Ukraine.

Spanish-speaking men hanging around there, lean and tall and with dark hair, appeal to me. Finally, I enter a Café and join H who is sitting at a table.

While we are talking L appears. I am shocked, afraid that H suspects me of having staged the encounter, of making it seem like a chance meeting. Both desperate and annoyed I signal to L that he is not welcome. At the same time I notice that he looks ill and miserable. His face is wrinkled and drawn, his skin spotted with sores. He hesitates, stricken, as if unable to believe this, and withdraws.

An encounter

I go up the stairs of the exit from a metro station. Emerging above ground I look around and notice a group of women in the adjacent park practising what is probably a martial art. There is another one close by. The participants move in sync as if to some inner music. On closer inspection their bodies are blown up with big bellies and wide hips on disproportionately thin legs. I am intrigued, but don't want to be caught staring. So I tear myself away.

As I walk on I feel liberated as if leaving behind all my troubles for good until I notice a man walking by my side. He says:

'Promise me never ever to pass on this photo.' My heart skips a beat. Will it be something horrible?

'Of course,' I burst out before I can look at it. Now, he is holding the photo in front of my eyes. It is a shot over the shoulder of another man with my companion in semi-profile, features contorted, and stumbling as if drunk or on drugs. He is in a very bad state.

Injury

The athlete`s face is contorted with pain from an injury. He looks very ill and can hardly stand upright. However, nobody dares talk to him to persuade him to withdraw from the tournament. If he does not step aside, his team won´t have any chance of success.

Brushing one´s teeth

I watch a man, H, brushing his teeth. They look healthy, all white. He goes about it very thoroughly, tackling each side from the incisors to the canines and the molars, tooth after tooth, the upper and the lower jaw. Now, he has finished, I think, but he starts a new cycle. I try to work out his system. Does he dedicate five minutes to each section all told? This is how it is done properly. By now, my admiration is tinged with a touch of impatience.

Poor Sasha March 4

It is on the bus to Stuttgart on a sunny day. My brother W is sitting in the row in front of me with his 13-year-old son. The row in front of them is occupied by four middle-aged men in red ski jackets looking tall and athletic. They are probably handsome. Each of them holds a pair of downhill skis so that they lean against a shoulder. When one of them turns around, I notice that he is older than expected with a heavily lined face and rotten teeth. Why on earth are they heading for Stuttgart at this time of day away from the ski areas? I wonder. Suddenly, I remember seeing them on one of the buses in the opposite direction, recently. Perhaps, they are on their way back from their skiing holiday, now.

My nephew turns around offering me fruits cut in half on a plate. They look like plums, only bigger. I decline politely, because I am afraid they are soft and fibrous and thus not refreshing. He, however, would like to be rid of them. Noticing his disappointment I feel sorry for him. Inadvertently and nonsensically, I call out:

'Poor Sasha!' Then we both burst out laughing.

At a town festival March 7

I am sitting in the middle of a long ale-bench surrounded by colleagues. In front of me is a text on an

A4 paper. It is a role play I am supposed to read out aloud. Without looking at it more closely, I pass it on to Ro. Instead of starting with the recital, he asks me a question, but I remain silent.

I take a bite from a pretzel half. A second half, which, however, is not its counterpart, is lying in front of me. At once, someone throws a handful of white powder into a big bowl of water on our table. It bubbles and boils. Hot steam rises. There is a flurry of shrieks and shouts as my colleagues are amazed and a little scared.

'If the powder is calcium oxide, that is, burnt lime, this is what happens,' I say reassuringly.

Unexpectedly, low, cold, short-lived flames in violet, orange and red emerge and flicker on the surface of the water in the bowl.[8] The bystanders ooh and aah and want to know the whys and wherefores.

'Perhaps the calcium oxide contained remnants of inflammable elementary calcium. This would explain the orange-red tinge of some of the flames. The other colours might indicate that ions of alkaline and alkaline earth metals were involved. Violet for potassium, yellow for sodium,' I explain

Later we are sitting on an ale-bank in the market square. Pretzel halves are piled up on a plate on the table. Strangely, there are quite a number of men walking around the square in well-worn jackets and trousers and with a rifle over their shoulder or in one

---

[8] I have never carried out this experiment. Both what I observed and how I explained it belong to the world of the dream.

of their hands. Some have gathered in groups, others are on their way to a shop or on an errand in the town hall or bank. They seem all busy. It is like in a town in the Wild West. I assume that they are dressed up like at a carnival or a theme party and remark humorously:

'Imagine that this is real. That everyone could carry a gun and you could shoot a rabbit or deer for dinner from time to time.'

All around me, indignant shouts of protest surge. These people are so easily provoked, I think and look at my two pretzel halves. They taste a bit dry.

On a train journey

I play a video game on a tablet computer. The fellow passenger sitting in the aisle seat beside me is watching. In order to propel the action forward I have to click on the figure in the scene which corresponds to the one given at the screen margin. Although I have spotted it, I hesitate, long enough for my neighbour to feel obliged to point it out to me. It is an animal reminiscent of a sheep. When I touch it with my finger, however, nothing happens. Suddenly, an image appears on the screen which does not have anything to do with the game. I try to close it in order to be able to go on playing, but it doesn't go away.

Am I going to fall in love with my fellow passenger? I like him. Now, he is getting up. He is heavier than I thought. Standing he leans over a little to rummage in the luggage rack under the roof. He is looking for a jacket, for something to put on when the mosquitoes attack.

'Mosquitoes?' I ask. 'Really?' I picture the situation. 'In Russia, perhaps?' I ask, laughing incredulously. 'Are we going to go so far?'

I make a mental search of my suitcase wondering if it contains anything that covers my whole body including my head. The only piece remotely suitable is a lilac knee-length winter jacket without a hood. I deem it insufficient and too warm to boot.

Meanwhile, the train has almost come to a halt. The carriage, which has lost its roof and walls, passes through a chemist's at walking pace. This makes it possible to reach for products at arm's length on the shelves. Though the box of tissues in my hand is nearly empty with just a third of its original content left, I am resolved not to do this, because it would be against my principles.

Speeding

I am driving along an almost deserted suburban street with only here and there a pedestrian on the pavement. When I am just about able to swerve in order to avoid brushing a woman, I become aware that I am speeding. Although I am skidding, now, and unable to keep the car on my side of the street, I don´t do anything to slow down.

A visit in Norwich   March 13

I am in a relatively small bedroom with a young man and a young woman I used to know in my year abroad at the University of East Anglia in Norwich. If it were them, however, they would be middle-aged with the man some years her senior.

While they are sitting on the double bed, I face the young couple from a chair in the cramped space in front of its lower end. In the course of our conversation I ask after our mutual friends. However, the man has not heard of them for a long time, and the young woman seems to be completely at a loss. I remind her that while studying at UEA, I attended the rehearsals and took part in a few performances of the Country Dancing Society. Some years later I visited Norwich again over a weekend during a stay in London and met them and a few other members I had been close to.

I hope that my account has put the young woman´s mind at ease. The man, however, makes a point in confirming that he has not had any contact with the Society, since then. Indeed, he has lost sight of them altogether, although he used to be a dedicated long-term member of the group. This makes me wonder.

After the rehearsal

It is during a rehearsal with Mr. D, my former music teacher, who is as young as he was while I was at school. We practise singing a song for several voices. The other participants are H, one of our girls and a child of Mr. D´s. It does not go well, but I like my voice, especially, when I sing the first few bars which run between a medium and a higher pitch. This has not occurred to me before. I hope Mr. D notices it, too: how beautiful my voice is and that I am talented.

Mr. D, however, is above all dissatisfied with our performance, and with the concert looming he suggests that we should stay till Friday, which means another two days. I decline spontaneously, well aware that H and our child are keen on getting home but won´t speak for themselves.

Now, we are sitting on the train passing through a rural area. It is pouring with rain. Raindrops are running by jerks diagonally across the carriage windows. Outside large patches in the fields are already flooded. A river winds between banks overgrown with shrubs and bushes. Its current is so strong that the water skips over the rocks in its bed and whirls on with white crests on its surface.

'It smells like spring,' says one of my fellow travellers. I breathe in deeply and close my eyes to be better able to taste its fragrance.

An incident in the foyer

After the concert I leave the hall with two friends, a couple. While we cross the lobby to the wardrobe, he is explaining the world to her. I overhear the thought that there was a Russian revolution before, a long time ago. When I look at her, I notice that she isn't feeling well and getting worse. In that moment she bends over to throw up on the spot. A puddle of vomit forms on the floor. The smell reaches my nose immediately. He remains standing beside her awkwardly while I walk on to the wardrobe feeling detached and wondering about it.

There I borrow cleaning equipment, a scrubbing brush with a bucket and a cleaning rag. The attendants at the wardrobe insist on my being paid for the work and ask for my personal data and the kind of wage I expect. To speed this up I propose 13 € willing to accept less if they object. Finally I am allowed to pick up my equipment and return to the site of the incident.

Not the right moment March 14

'... why on earth did she choose this moment to become pregnant?' says a woman to another woman in a matter-of-fact tone neither reproachfully nor compassionately nor even in amazement.

An incriminating photo March 16

W and I are sitting at a table with a colleague of mine, when a sequence of photos in the folder lying open in front of the latter catches my eye. The one at the top features H and me at a moment of intimacy. I am shaken deep inside. My colleague claims that I sent the photos to him with an e-mail. Never would I do such a thing, but apparently, the proof is on the table. Why did he file the photos, anyway? I wonder, but how this could be an exonerating circumstance escapes me. I am afraid that there will be no way to make H believe me.

Hungry March 21

I descend the flight of stairs to the ground floor of a late 19th century town house and step on the pavement. My neighbour´s blue van is parked at the kerb.

Crossing over I notice that the sliding doors looking towards the street are open. He offers baguette and big red sausages. I am grateful because I am hungry and pull off a sizeable piece from the loaf. As it still seems to be too small I tear off another, though smaller piece and hope that I don't come across as greedy. Now for the sausage. To my disappointment there is no smell, nor can I discover a barbecue anywhere. Trying to come to terms with the conclusion that there are no sausages, after all, I have a brainwave. The steam escaping from the electric kettle on the floor might be a clue that they are in there. I open the lid and reach for a sausage, but now I don't have enough hands to arrange the three items in such a way that I would be able to eat in a civilized manner. However, in spite of the sausage and the smaller piece of bread in my right hand I can still use my fingers to tear open the bigger piece of bread I am holding in my left. Though I manage without dropping any of the said items, I go about it so clumsily that I end up with a zig-zag shaped crumbly cavern. At last, I am able to insert the sausage and clear the way for the next customer.

A spectacle

It is during a walk in a park. Not far ahead on my right a crowd has gathered around a cone-shaped hill with a flat top. Some people are standing in a row on a platform up there surrounded by a chain-link fence. I gather that this is part of a victory ceremony after a beer-drinking competition. The winner, who is standing on a winner´s podium, is a young man with his hair in a ponytail. He lifts both arms and waves in celebration. The spectators clap and cheer.

Suddenly, he jumps off pulling up his knees from his standing position, but fails to vault the fence. Instead, he lands right in front of it. With what looks like a desperate effort he hurls himself on the fence and climbs it. As it yields to his weight he struggles till he has straddled it, his face twisted with the pain from the thin wire pressed against his behind. I hover between pity and doubt. There is an almost comical side to his labours. Can it just be part of a show?

Then he lets himself drop on the other side. Back on his feet, he builds up momentum by turning around with his lowered right arm out-stretched and flings an object towards a nearby patch of park overgrown with bushes. So he is an artiste, after all, I wonder. At the end of the arc of its trajectory the object hits the ground with a dark vibrating bang. A glowing white shape – looking like a big stapler - rises to the sky.

Again the man puts his hand into his pocket and flings something. When the pea-like objects hit the ground, smaller fireworks erupt. Light bubbles rise and then hover for a while silently under the canopy of clouds.

In Spain   March 24

I am on my way to a memorial across dry, rock-strewn countryside. My destination is the grave of Luana and Maria[9] with its plaque informing visitors about their fate. On the passenger seat of the hired car there is so little space that the right half of my body sticks out at the side.

After the visit I am taken to a hall. Inside an association dedicated to the memory of Maria and Luana has gathered. Somebody passes me a microphone, and I use it to say:

'Thank you for the music.' Everyone laughs.

The permit   March 26

In a school building. I am a senior pupil going downstairs with some waste paper in my left hand. The caretaker, who is coming my way from downstairs, is carrying a bin. When I make to drop the paper into it, he swerves and moves it out of reach.

'You have to fill in a permit, first,' he says. Annoyed, not least with myself, because I should have done this long ago, I join him on his way to his cubicle. There, I fill in a form at the service hatch and pay a

---

[9] They do not correspond to anyone in the real world.

deposit. Now, I can dispose of the waste paper. Besides, I buy a cheese sandwich. When I receive it, I am disappointed because it is so small, with a slice only the size of a third of a loaf.

Besides, both the bread and the cheese are of an artificial orange. Not exactly good value for money, I think. Not wanting to be rude, however, I resist the urge to make a critical or even a gently ironic remark and take the sandwich with me to the school canteen. There at a table I discover a friend with a fried egg in front of her. Surprisingly, she has bought another one for me, which makes me feel glad, but I am also afraid that together with the sandwich it will be more than plenty.

Feeling guilty

In a school building with an open central staircase. Something is lying on the head of the stairs. It could be any piece of paper. On closer inspection it turns out to be an envelope I must have dropped earlier without noticing. Glad and relieved to have found it, I bend down to pick it up.

After straightening myself I am about to head downstairs, when I see a colleague mounting the stairs towards me. Our eyes meet unexpectedly, and I catch her reproachful look. It causes a hot surge of guilt to flood my whole body. But I pass by her without stopping to talk.

House cleaning   March 28

Many helpers are busy cleaning my parents´ house. It appears to be bigger than I remember. We have almost finished. I am on the ground floor where I notice some dirt that has been overlooked on the first two steps of the staircase. Eager to prove my diligence, I say to R, the senior colleague, who approaches me sweeping the stairs from above:

'I´m going to deal with this,' but she does not hear me or why does she go on as if she hasn´t heard my offer? Feeling unrightfully overlooked I watch her but refrain from speaking for myself. It hurts, but anyway, she is the boss.

An ending

I look out of the dormer window of our house in St. Georgen over the Brigach valley, which stretches like a big tub towards the horizon until it is bounded by a range of hills in the distance. The sky is overcast with low-hanging clouds. It is dark like after sunset although it is early afternoon. I glance at my watch to dispel my doubts.

I am standing in a big loft. The enveloping roof, a light wooden structure, conveys a friendly and hospitable atmosphere. Apart from the living room suite of the same light wood as the roof, the room is sparsely furnished. A square photobook featuring a Black Forest farmhouse on its cover is lying on the coffee table. F was drawn to the landscapes in it. I didn´t expect him to return it so soon. Is he really seeing someone else? I have come to know him so well by now and could be a good partner. Perhaps, it is just wishful thinking that I sensed affection and regret in his manner just now.

Sunday

One warm, sunny Sunday H, our children in their teens and I are on a bike tour. Our destination is a restaurant in the country where we are going to have lunch. We are almost there. We are on the main road through the village leaving the bridge across the river to our right while cycling along a ninety-degree bend. There in front of us is the restaurant.

A sleepless night   March 29

I spend the night mostly awake and in pain. The small of my back and my left hip joint are hurting. Besides, I am troubled by anxious thoughts about a coming meeting with two mothers. In the end I must have fallen asleep at some time. On waking up I see my father´s face in my mind´s eye and draw comfort from his familiar roguish smile.

A mysterious car   April 4

A big black sedan car emerges from the mouth of an underground car park and glides uphill towards the pavement. The intersection with the sidewalk is cordoned off with red and white tape and guarded by a police officer or security guard.

I am one in a crowd waiting for the car to pass. In the meantime, I glean snippets of the surrounding conversations. There is a murmur that the car contains carrier pigeons. Other voices claim that it belongs to a Russian but are doubtful about the carrier pigeons.

An English lesson

I am standing in front of the barrier, impatient because my pupils are waiting on a square on its other side. I am supposed to give them an English lesson with a senior staff member in attendance. However, I am ill prepared. The text book on the desk is unfamiliar to me. Nor can I remember the faces and names of my pupils. Having to call them up by pointing at them deeply embarrasses me. The subject of the lesson turns out to be a difficult poem, obscure even to me. I try to remain in control by asking students to read out some lines, but they keep struggling and stumbling. They take ages and by the end of the lesson we have hardly made any progress.

Not the right outfit   April 4

It is time to leave for a concert, which I, as a young adult, take part in. This means interrupting my work, filing my notes and stowing the folder away in my shelf. Time passes and I haven´t changed, yet. Finally I am ready. I wear a T-shirt and very short tight shorts exposing the upper fleshy part of my thighs. It feels uncomfortable and embarrassing. Am I really supposed to go on the stage like this? In passing I open a desk drawer and reach for a double reed in case I am expected to play the oboe, but I can´t find any. Never mind. I didn't even attend the rehearsals. So they'll be fine without me. I close the door, and we, my mother, daughter J and I ride to the ground floor of the block of flats in the lift and walk to the tram stop.

While waiting for the tram to the city centre in the middle of a wide avenue, I decide that my outfit is unsuitable for the occasion. After all, the venue is a late 19th century Neo-Gothic church. So my mother and J get on the tram without me, while I am hurrying back to the block of flats to change into different clothes.

Turning into the backstreet where it is located, I face the weather-worn concrete facades like a visitor unsure which entrance to take. Only then do I remember having to pass by number 5 at the front to get to number 7 at the back. I learn that the lift is concealed behind a mirrored wall. The door will open when it arrives, but with no buttons to call it I have to wait. Time is running out. There is no chance of arriving at the church in time.

Finally, I have changed. Now, I wear a white T-shirt and a colourfully patterned red skirt. As its design does not match the shape of my body, it hangs on my hips like a sack and thus makes me look rather plump, but I tell myself that it'll have to do. By now, J has returned, too. Her outfit resembles mine in design and colour, and we are ready to set out to the tram stop for the second time.

Sudden death

Mama descends to our ground floor flat and tells me that Grandma has died. I am caught off guard, although, as I suddenly remember now, it was to be expected she wouldn't survive, because she was injured so badly in an accident recently.

A phone call   April 4

During a holiday in England I, about 18 years old, call home from a telephone box. Grandma picks up the receiver. Her long silences between short and hesitant replies convey her displeasure more than words could. My heart is heavy. She is right. I haven't been in touch for over two weeks. Nonetheless, I don't apologize, but go on talking as if I didn't notice.

A snack

In the kitchen. On the work surface in front of me is the thick crescent of a pretzel. I open the fridge and reach for butter and apricot jam.

An acquaintance

On a cupola-shaped mountain top in summer. I have
just set out for the descent on a serpentine path, when
I pass by a man. In a joyful moment of certain recog-
nition my eyes rest on his face. It is enveloped by a
full grizzled beard, and a halo of fluffy grey hair
frames his head. I used to know him in Freiburg, but
I can't remember for the world who and what he was
exactly. When I greet him he remains unfazed as if we
were total strangers.

Sailing

I have been spending some days with a female friend
in a holiday cottage at a bay somewhere by the sea. It
is our final day. Over the last hour clouds have accu-
mulated. It is low tide just about to turn and to start
coming in with a thundering surge. A strong wind is
tearing at my clothes. I am at the beach looking at the
wooden boat lying in the wet sand in front of me. It
has a rickety makeshift mast, a wooden pole, on
which a big piece of cloth is fluttering. If only we
could fasten it to make it work as a sail. How easily
and swiftly we would fly over the rough sea. But the
cloth is too soft, not proper canvas. It keeps fluttering

erratically in the wind, and I am unable to catch and contain it.

Now my friend, on whose assistance I have counted, is passing by. Although she must have seen me, she walks on as if I weren't there. Following her with my eyes, I see that she has grown plump with her thighs appearing thick and shapeless in the black leggings she is wearing. Maybe it is because she stopped running that she has lost her athletic looks, I wonder.

Campaigning   April 8

The setting is a stadium somewhere in Poland where a convention on democracy and its acceptance takes place. I am about to give a presentation on the fuel cell technology and the production of hydrogen through electrolysis of water. As I have been quite immersed in my subject, I only start to realize that the mood in the stadium has turned and that the atmosphere around me is becoming more and more hostile. So I am glad when men in dark green tracksuit tops with black and white trimmings appear and offer me their protection. They escort me through the crowd and lead me out of the stadium.

At the baker's   April 9

Customers are standing in front of the counter at the baker's. They block the view of the front page of the tabloid *Bild* spread out there. Thus, I am unable to get a glimpse of the banner headline I would so much like to read.

Lagging behind   April 10

I am close to the upper terminus of a ski lift or cable car. Fog is hovering low above the snow-covered mountain landscape. I stand beside a cross-country track which only extends a few metres before it is swallowed by whiteness. The two little girls have a head start, and I still struggle to sort out my stuff. With a senior colleague just gliding past, I pull myself together and decide to leave a few smaller objects that are not mine behind in the snow next to the track. I am aware that this doesn't make sense because the owners mightn't even pass by. But after putting on my skis I can finally set out, too.

Nuns

It is in a village in a valley on a sunny summer Sunday morning. The church bells ring calling the parishioners to the service. I am standing by a footbridge over a narrow river, when two young women dressed in black pass me by. Nuns on their way to church, I think. As they don't wear long grey dresses and white bonnets, they can't be protestant sisters. Taking a closer look, it strikes me that one of the women is dressed in a short skirt with inlaid lace above black nylon tights.

She lives out her love of fashion, I conclude, and it leaves me bewildered that nuns can evidently take this liberty.

Holiday plans

I am sitting on the floor leaning against the wall of one side of a big room. On the other side H and his brother are talking with each other in very low voices. I am waiting anxiously for their verdict hoping that they are going to forgive me. Now, his brother turns to me. He announces that in the summer they are going to visit some signature towns of rural Bavaria, Oberammergau among them, and asks if I would like to join them. My gut-feeling is that this will be terribly boring. Nevertheless, I sound excited when, despite myself, I consent immediately.

'I have been to Lech am Arlberg,' I add enthusiastically, well aware that this is in Austria. 'It´s a beautiful place.'

In my mind´s eye I see a mountain landscape with the tops covered by snow. An inviting path leads uphill across pastures from which the edges of rocks peek out here and there. I am eager to immerse myself in this landscape, but suspect that my male companions shy away from such an effort.

'You can drive up there and set out from the car park,' I say pre-empting the possible objection that this would imply too much exertion. I desist from making fun of them, however, because for one I am glad to be forgiven and besides, I second-guess that H´s brother hides his doubts of not being fit enough behind his coolness. What appears certain though is the downside of teaming up with them, which is, that I will have to tame my love of adventure in the great outdoors.

Who is in charge?   11. April

One of the stops of our staff outing is a museum. I learn that you can choose between an earlier and a later date for a guided tour and look around for a person with a clipboard, who is in charge of the reservations. Re has just emerged in the door of one of the buildings and joins us in the courtyard, but she does not seem to be the one in charge. On the fringe of our crowd Ma bends over An´s back using it for support to write something down. I am sure, however, that the list of participants is not on his pad.

A steep climb

We set out on inline skates. S says that Lisa, her 9-year-old granddaughter, who I can see in the corner of my eye, is already very clever at skating.

'So is J,' I reply. Only then do I realize that J is riding her bike. I let Lisa and J overtake us. The road, which has lead uphill for a while, becomes steeper.

'You won´t make it to the top,' says S goading me on to a challenge.

By degrees, it gets harder to retain the momentum for gliding upwards, and it costs more and more effort. My eyes are focused on the path on which leaves in shining yellow, orange and red are laid out, each separately, neither soiled nor torn by footsteps, pristine as if newly fallen.

Finally, the ongoing steep rise forces me to give up skating and to climb further upwards laboriously step by step with the skates on my feet.

The right medication

It is on a staff outing. A narrowing of the footpath causes us to walk in pairs. My partner tells me about some medicine he once took. He is not going to do it again ever, he says, because after half an hour he was totally knocked out.

All at once I am holding two drip bottles of medicine in one hand. As the lids are missing I go on holding them upright wondering what to do with them and if one of them contains my medication. In the end I taste the one my colleague has likely referred to and wait for the effect to kick in.

Is it going to be similarly strong? I wonder.

Before the race   April 13

A man opens the side door to the riding hall and enters. The door closes behind him. After a while I see him leaving the hall through the stable door on the far side leading a horse with a jockey in a brightly yellow jerkin on its back. Behind them walks a second man with a horse and then another man with a horse and a jockey. I admire the first man because he is a self-made man who grew up in modest circumstances whereas the one at the back has always been cushioned by the family assets. It is not due to his own achievements that he is able to afford a jockey. The man in the middle in turn was unable to maintain his social status. He has to ride his horse himself.

Final math exam

It's the final exam in maths. Two books with exam questions, a red one and a blue one, are handed out to us besides matching notebooks for the solutions. Although he is not a pupil at my grammar school, F is taking the exam, too.

With a touch of recklessness I consciously open the blue book, although I am assigned the set of questions in the red one. I am quite certain that I can still tackle them, later. I get absorbed quickly, and thus focused on my work, I make great progress filling the pages of the blue notebook with what I am sure to be viable solutions. Driven even more by my sense of achievement I go on and on. Whenever I think of the tasks I have actually been assigned, I postpone starting to work on them.

When with an act of will I finally open the red book, there is only half an hour left. Though aware that this won't be enough, I hope that with my mind working as it has so far, I'll get a sizeable part of it done. However, after a good start with some easy problems I begin to struggle and get out of step. Now I am stuck with a task that baffles me so much that I move on to the next one. Yet, I am not able to solve it, either. To top it all, I have mislaid the red book. Time passes and I am losing my nerve.

The scene has changed. I am not in the exam hall any more, but sitting at a desk in a long narrow room covered with a lot of papers and books. Next to me is one of my senior pupils. She edges closer and closer until her upper body presses against me, which infuriates me. I shove her away with the weight of my left shoulder and arm in order to stop her from copying my solutions.

Now, time is out and I have embarrassingly few results. I'll get a bad mark well below my true skills and expectations. This won't be an obstacle to me graduating from high school, though. After all, the math exam is only a small part of the requirements.

'Shouldn't we have long posted our exam papers?' I ask, but my question remains unanswered.

A glance at the clock reminds me that it is time for the class photo. I hurry off, leaving everything behind. The first group I pass by is my extended family dominated by elderly adults in their summer Sunday best. Mama stands out in her yellow, white and grey check lady's suit. I wonder what might be the occasion of this gathering. Trying to make myself as invisible as possible I slink past at the back worried that I might already be late for the photo. So I am relieved when the group emerging behind them indeed prove to be my schoolmates arranged for the photo. On my approach some figures break loose. Has the photo already been taken without me? I would really mind not being in it.

The end of summer   15. April

It is a dark, almost black night. There is only a glimmer of light from the surface of the lake at the edge of my home town, which I ride by on my bike. Summer is over, and I don´t regret that the water isn´t warm enough for swimming, any more.

Sister and brother

I am lying on my bed in my childhood room with my laptop open in front of me when I hear a creaking and cracking from the attic room above me. A is going to bed, there. I just want to be left alone and resent him being so close.

All at once he is in the upper storey of my bunkbed with no ceiling between us, any more. My nerves are on edge, but I know that I have to resign myself to this new situation. Then, he is suddenly lying beside me in my bed. I am about to check my e-mails but desist and close my laptop, because he can see the screen. In order to make clear that it is time to go to sleep, I turn over away from him, but remain wide awake because he keeps fidgeting and occasionally rummages around on the floor beside his bed, once, I suspect, taking care of a pair of wet bathing trunks.

Meanwhile, I must have been asleep. Although I am tired out like in the middle of a sleepless night, it is actually daylight, when I hear him pottering around in the room. His little daughter is tottering about, too. She is between two and three years old with her bottom covered by a diaper.

In the toy department

Now, A and I are in a shopping centre with our children M and C. Seeing them together it strikes me what a baby M still is. C is actually the same age as her cousin, but behaves like an older and more mature child. We hang around in the children´s department between generously arranged shelves and islands on the floor covered with toys. C asks if we could go to the big doll´s house. I am ready, and glad to have a destination. We head there ambling through the vast showrooms on our way.

Open day

It is the open day at the university hospital in Stuttgart. They offer guided tours. I am on the premises walking towards a lookout tower[10]. Some visitors

---

[10] The location does not correspond to the one in the real world.

with their guide in front have just left it and are passing by me. I consider joining them, but wonder if I
should as I don´t have a ticket, and they are already
heading for their last stop, the training facilities for
the state examination candidates. Apparently, I wear
my heart on my sleeve, as a member of the group, a
man in a trench coat, encourages me to join them. He
says I look like a teacher and as such would of course
be interested in getting to know the institute. He is a
vivacious windy type, a will-o´-the-wisp hurrying
hither and thither and somehow impossible to grasp.
I wonder if we haven´t met before, but he evades me
and carries on elsewhere in the group.

Later, I climb the lookout tower in the company of
a young Asian woman and the man in the trench coat.
It is surrounded by an English garden, a vast green
area dotted with giant old trees and a white gazebo in
the classical Greek style on a hill. On my way down
the winding stairs taper and turn into a tube made of
translucent pink perspex shimmering like rose
quartz. It has become so narrow that it almost clings
to me and I can slide through it gently to the bottom.
I wait outside for the Asian woman wondering if she
is able to give herself up to the tube. When she
emerges soon after, we agree to grab a bite at a café
nearby. The man in the trench coat is already scurry-
ing ahead heralding our arrival in the outside seating
area.

Now, he is talking to a waiter and I overhear him
asking about someone. Then he confronts a young
dark-skinned man, whom I recognize as V, a senior

student of mine. He grabs him by the collar of his shirt and in a bout of aggressive exuberance lifts him, apparently without any great effort, until he is at eye level with him and then higher above his head. I am deeply sorry for the victim and wonder about the significance of this demonstration of power veiled in benevolence.

A memorial service 17 April

Mourners have gathered for the memorial service of a deceased colleague of mine in a modern, spacious church flooded with light. Some are sitting in the pews, others are standing scattered around the nave. A few staff members are supposed to recite tributes to the deceased written by our pupils. I wonder why they don´t do this themselves. Perhaps they are too sad, too upset and afraid of breaking down while reading. Anyway, I don´t mind. Convinced of my reciting skills and my good voice I look forward to accomplishing this task.

The vice head teacher hands out the sheets of notepad paper covered on both pages with handwriting in different colours, so many, that I ask myself how long it will take to read all this out. Is this even appropriate?

A female colleague is standing at the door to an adjoining hall, a hub from which more rooms and corridors branch off. She says that I ought to take one of the pills from the table in the room to make sure I won't transmit a disease I might have. Thinking of her partner who is a cancer patient I study the assortment of blister strips. To my surprise they don't contain small white pills but capsules. Nor are they just one kind but some are yellow and some are purple, which baffles me even more. Anxious to find the right ones I look for clues and finally hold samples against the light to inspect the powder inside them. Still, I am incapable of making an informed decision. In the end, I press out one capsule randomly just to be able to join the funeral service.

Back in the pew I overhear one of the speakers citing my father's name as if he were a well-known source of worldly wisdom, but, alas, the context has escaped me. How has she heard about him and what exactly has she come to know? I wonder. After all, he was an ordinary man all his life. I listen attentively but in vain. She has long changed the subject.

The outhouse

C and I walk down a steep hill and make a detour to a public toilet. It turns out to be just a single cubicle, so narrow that it is almost impossible to squeeze in.

Besides, you have to pull yourself up through a tube made of yellow polyurethane to get to the bowl. I give C a leg up and watch her feet dangling until she has disappeared. Then, I wait outside, and after a while she re-emerges. Now, it´s my turn, but hard as I try, I can´t reach high enough to find somewhere to hold on to and slip off each time. Finally, I give up, dejected and conscious that we have wasted a lot of time.

Back outside I take a closer look at our surroundings. Further downhill I discover steep cliffs and between them people on a beach. The sight cheers me up and fills me with a sense of adventure.

'This is where we want to go,' I say. 'We just have to fetch Daddy, first.'

He is sitting further uphill on the grass waiting for us and wondering about our whereabouts. We tell him about the toilet.

Not one of them

We are staying at a hostel. It is evening, and I go down the iron stairs to the ground floor wondering which is the door to the kitchen. I opt for the most likely and it is a hit. Inside W and C are busy cooking a meal together. Besides, two or three young adults are hanging around. The vibes I pick up, however, make me feel like the stranger in the room. Apparently, they have somehow agreed that I don´t fit in. Their body language is expressive of their contempt for me, which makes me feel extremely uncomfortable, deeply hurt even.

Finally, I summon the courage to ask why they always dissuade me from joining them when they go out in the evenings. One of them explains that there was this lecture by a linguist in Czech, which they were obliged to attend. With linguistics being a *ubicund*[11] discipline, which means that they are exploring the principles languages have in common, it wasn't an option to stay away. No doubt this is a shady excuse. He hasn't even answered my question. Besides, I did not mean this specific evening, but all the other occasions when they went out together.

Breakfast at the youth club   April 18

On my way to school I go by the youth club on the outskirts of the small town, which is a detour. I have a cherry and custard gateau from a recipe of my mother's with me. Yet, it has already been eaten into and only the middle section is left. I expect L to join me there. Indeed, he arrives soon after, and I eat some of the gateau for breakfast. It tastes delicious, but I feel a little taken aback because he declines, when I offer some to him. When it is time for me to leave, I would

---

[11] This is a fantasy word.

like to kiss him farewell. He seems to be taken by surprise, and so it is only a cold and cursory kiss.

Outside, the snow-covered surroundings envelop me. On entering the small town, I have to pass a check point. Walking on, the layer of snow on the sidewalk becomes so thick that I can skate down to the school. This feels liberating and makes me happy.

There are no sign posts in the entrance hall. Uncertain as I am about where to turn, I am glad when some pupils offer to escort me through the barren corridors with their forbidding concrete walls to the secretary´s office. They introduce me as a new pupil. I feel quite at home.

Closed

It is a dark night. A woman parks her car in front of the indoor swimming pool. There are no lights on in the building. When she realizes that it is closed, she is deeply disappointed.

'It happens to all of us,' I say to comfort her. On starting the engine to drive off again, she notices that one of her rear tyres is flat.

A letter   April 23

C has sent me a long hand-written letter containing passages of dialogue. I read between the lines that she is struggling and regret that I have failed to see this until now.

May to August 2022

A ride on the bus   May 1

In the Black Forest with C as a little girl. We are walking down a path, her little hand in mine. Our destination is a bus station, and I am afraid that we'll miss the bus, but suddenly we are able to skate on our shoes and cover the final leg of our walk effortlessly.

The bus is standing at the bus stop about to leave. Some last-minute passengers are hurrying to the doors. When I put my foot on the footboard, however, the doors are closing. I make an effort to squeeze in between them wondering about the bus driver, who ignored me so blatantly, but I fail and the bus just pulls away. I hold on to the door hoping that he will see me presently and stop to let me in, but in vain. Despite my misgivings about the dangers I hang on. It is a strain on my biceps, but to my surprise it is not unbearable. I can keep on like this for some time longer. Besides, I can see houses on the horizon. This must be the next village, and the bus will certainly stop there.

Exam day   May 15

It is the day of my exams both in chemistry and later in physics. I am in my childhood home. The front door bell is ringing. On opening a number of my teacher colleagues crowd in. Ms N, who ran my trainee teacher´s course in chemistry, is among them. I lead them upstairs into the flat on the first floor and let them out onto the balcony expecting that they will appreciate the view.

On the railing an iron grid is fastened. Some of my colleagues have climbed up and are hanging there, now. A young woman is even sitting on the topmost horizontal bar with her hands closed around it, leaning back nonchalantly and with her legs dangling. Shocked by this sight I plead with her to climb down to a safer place, but she only laughs and lolls around some more. It seems to me, however, that she does adjust her position a little to make sure she won´t lose control.

I am supposed to gather some bowls and glasses for the practical exam and am embarrassed not to be able to provide sets of identical pieces. Instead they have different shapes, sizes and colours. I discard the most unsuitable ones, among them flat dishes with their floor upwardly curved.

Still in search of the required laboratory equipment I hit upon a man and a woman sitting around a coffee table in leather arm chairs in a converted cellar room. Are they my examiners? They do not notice me. It is as if I were invisible.

When I step out of the front door, I bump into a youth, who asks me reproachfully where I have been. The exam commission have been waiting, and here I am hanging around procrastinating.

'That´s normal. Everyone does it.' I reply and go back into the house to face my examiners. On the assumption that the exam is going to take place in the attic, I resolve to ask the commission not to make me carry out experiments with the gas burner, there.

In the library   15 May

Before the scheduled departure we are encouraged to borrow some books from the library. Stop bars on the floor in front of the counter indicate the position of the customers next in line. In this area wearing a face mask is mandatory. Luckily, I find one in my pocket and put it on fumbling with my glasses.

An elderly couple, a man and a woman, are standing at the counter. The man is holding up an oblong plastic frame vertically. It is divided into two equal sections by a metal rod between the lengths. He and his partner are amused about an incident that has just passed. While making as if to congratulate the couple, the middle-aged woman with red hair standing in the background, now, kissed the man through the upheld frame on his lips. The couple are still chuckling in recollection. An embarrassing accident. After all he did not hold up the frame to this purpose, the man gasps. All present are aware, however, that the red-haired woman is painfully in love with him.

At the counter it turns out that two of the titles I have selected are actually volumes from the *Bibi Blocksberg* series, but with a different book cover. I summon up all my courage to say that I have taken them out of the shelf by accident and that I would like to return them. Now, I have only two English language training books left which, considering my advanced language skills, won´t be a satisfactory pastime. Compared to my fellow travellers who I can see carrying four to five books to the counter, I am very poorly equipped for the journey. If I get bored I can write something, I reassure myself, but I am not entirely convinced.

A bus is supposed to take us on a twenty-kilometre ride overland to our destination. While the passengers are getting on it by and by, two pupils split off from the group and start walking along the road. Soon they fall into a jog trot. Do they really mean to run the 20 kilometres? Or do they count on the bus catching up and stopping for them? In that case they won´t be able to cover a lot of ground.

A new beginning

H and I approach a group of people. They are musicians about to unpack their instruments. He has met them recently and is upbeat about cooperating with them, thus launching a new beginning.

Inspection   May 16

While I am looking for something in the chemistry laboratory at my school and tidying up my trolley-table
at the same time, a school supervisor walks past in-
specting the rooms. She is escorted by another, male
official. I address her respectfully meaning to pass on
an important piece of information. On receiving the
message, however, she only nods non-committally
and walks on.

Torn

On entering the hall where the party takes place I am
proud of my beautiful dress. When I look down at it,
however, I discover that the bottommost flounce has
partly come unstuck leaving a gaping tear. I try to pull
it up and make it stick but doubt that it will hold onto
the skirt for long.

In the course of the evening I overhear a couple taking their leave to search for their adolescent child. H
says deadpan:

'There is nothing like such a search, when it comes
to welding partners in a marriage together.' With a
sense of relief I reply:

'I am so glad that the lost child is not J.'

History   May 21

A big poster board leaning vertically against a wall
features a time line of historical periods. Next to the
explanations the sculpted heads of dogs protrude
from the board. They stand for the rulers who shaped
the era. All the heads look the same and are reminiscent of a Labrador Retriever´s but dappled with orange and red.

Birthday

By a frozen lake in winter with a new young colleague. The car is cluttered with stuff. It takes so much
time and effort to get hold of my skates and to put
them on that I almost give up. When I am finally on
the ice I glide along smoothly if not elegantly. Soon, I
have to share the space with more and more skaters,
which grates on my nerves. Yet, I adapt to the circumstances and get by.

Meanwhile I have joined a group of people sitting
by the lake. My colleague approaches and awards me
something like a coat of arms on a staff, which reminds me of the ones carried by standard bearers in
parades. It is made of an egg-shaped grid with strings
of pearls dangling inside. I must have looked baffled
thus causing the bystanders to call out:

'But it´s your birthday today!'

I beam with joy.

Listening to music   May 5

I, around 20 years old, am about to pull up my jeans, when F enters. I am embarrassed and flush with the effort to close the button and the zip, but when he is unexpectedly gracious I relax. He asks for a specific CD, which I hand over to him. We end up listening to it together. So does this mean that he has forgiven me? All the time I pray that he won´t hit upon the tender pieces I discovered on it the last time it was on without being able to remember how they got there.

Family life

My school friend X is sitting in her family´s living room with her parents. They are watching *Dallas* on TV. I have just arrived and stand near the door next to the sofa waiting for her to get up and go out with me. Suddenly I sense something brushing my hip. Looking down I see her father´s arm draped over the back rest his hand uncomfortably close. I make two steps sideways to get out of reach uncertain if this happened by accident.

During a summer night in a forest

It is a dark but mild summer´s night. I walk through a forest down a terraced hillside. After a while I rest on a plateau. I look around taking in the sounds and smells, when I hear a rustling. On closer inspection I see the black, narrow behind of an animal sticking out from a burrow in the hillside, while digging itself deeper into the ground. A badger. I return to the next plateau higher up. There I encounter the very same scene. A second badger. Tonight the badgers are active, I think.

A power cut   June 4

During an in-house training at my school, which involves work with computers, I pop outside and walk to the intersection of walkways at the edge of the school premises. There, I pull a flush-mounted socket board out of the ground and remove the plug, but realize immediately that this means a power cut in the whole school. In my mind´s eye I see screens going black, work in progress lost. So I plug it in again hoping that no-one noticed, that very short power cuts like this can somehow be bridged. Do I have to confess? It wouldn´t do not to. I am scared. And what if it came to light, anyway? I resolve to check out first if there was an impact at all and walk back towards the school building.

Late   June 5

It is time to set out for a meeting at school, but I would like to finish marking the exam paper in front of me first. This leads to me arriving late. When on entering I sense the questioning, slightly irritated looks of my colleagues, I show the exam paper to the chair. It is red with underlinings and comments in the margin, and I make a remark on frequently occurring mistakes like the incorrect usage of the present progressive.

Meanwhile I have sat down among my colleagues. Between the room documents in front of me is another sheet of paper, a page from my creative writing project. The right and left margins of the top half of the page are missing and only the middle is left. There isn´t much of a product to boast of, just chaotic scribblings, but I am confident about being able to go on from there and to turn it into something.

Satisfaction

It is by the Museum of Fine Arts in Basel. Some tourists turn to me to enquire after an exhibition that features important works by Böll[12].

'Isn't it divided between two museums?' they ask. Enthusiastically and with eloquence, I recommend the selection in the Museum of Fine Arts.

Proud of being so useful and of being able to give expert advice, I return to F who has been waiting for me in a niche around the corner. When I draw closer to him, my nose brushes his face by accident. He pulls away as if in disgust, and I step back, too, hurt and conscious that this might signify the end of our relationship.

A red currant cake   June 6

This red currant cake looks perfect, tempting to the utmost. The rim has risen above the rest of the surface. The cake is still whole, so that the inside is hidden from view, but I see it in my mind's eye and in anticipation, I taste the sour fruitiness of the red currants tempered by the sweet, smooth batter and the crumbly, firm base with its faint aroma of vanilla.

---

[12] Here, a fantasy artist.

After skiing

After some hours of downhill skiing A turns up with a Christmas pudding on a baking tray. He digs into it with a fork, raises a big chunk to his mouth and chews. That he can't wait until we sit around a table together sets my teeth on edge. Now our father drags himself upstairs. He looks ill.

'I have lugged back his pair of skis,' says A.

Feeling guilty because it escaped me that Papa needed help, I support him while he lowers himself to the floor and lies down. When I stroke his cheek tenderly, his head lolls about, and I am overcome by fear that he might die. But he smiles and says he is already much better. A ventures:

'He has only overstretched himself.'

Anniversary

At first, it seems like a reunion of my graduation class. I take part for the first time.

'You just haven't bothered, so far,' says one of the relatively stout middle-aged men I meet. I don't deny it.

Scanning the guests, I am unable to recognize the teenagers we used to be in the faces of these older adults. Nor can I remember their names. They all seem to be dressed up. The women are wearing loose, flowing robes with their hair done up in voluminous coiffures. They seem unnaturally tall as if standing on a flat pedestal.

A petite, grey-haired, elderly woman stands out among the crowd. Her clothes indicate that she is a parson, which makes me assume that I am attending an anniversary of my confirmation. Why has she come? I wonder, considering how unruly some of my classmates were. These people are important to her, I conclude. She belongs here.

Looking past the bystanders I see couples dancing. I would like to dance, too, and look around for a suitable partner. Mo, a classmate, catches my eye. He is sitting alone on a bench, but he is out of the question. Although he used to be charming in his way, he was often in deep trouble both at school and outside of it. Now, I recognize Bo, who was both charming and cultured, but am prevented from approaching him by a group of young men closing in and making lewd remarks.

Meanwhile, the setting has morphed into a playground. I sneak away from my pursuers and pull myself up a climbing frame. From above I am able to push off some of them causing them to lose their footing and to tumble down. But the last one, a comparatively little man, almost like a boy, has grabbed my leg in falling. Frantically, I try to shake him off. In vain.

Blood

I sense a trembling and gurgling in my left breast. Now I see brown stains on the carpet. Blood, I realize. Where does it come from? Then, I notice that it´s me who is bleeding, that the blood runs down the insides of my legs and drops in lumps onto the carpet where, gradually absorbed, it spreads. This is impossible, I think. After all, I have already gone through menopause. Does this mean that I am ill? Fatally ill? Someone is with me, a woman. She looks after me and her voice is humming softly at my ear.

The blue and white book   June 12

I am in the entrance hall of a central university building, probably at the University of Konstanz. Somehow I have got hold of a book in the A4 format with a blue and white cover, an exhibition catalogue, perhaps, or a political manifesto of the student union. I leaf through it, read a few headings, then the table of contents, but I am unable to make head or tail of it. Suddenly it falls open at a page with a big kitchen knife and another object pasted onto it. That´s art, I think.

I want to remove the knife before throwing the book into the waste paper basket, but then change my mind. What if anyone finds the knife on me? I might be suspected of planning something. So I put the book with the knife inside into the bin. Another copy with its blue and white cover is already there.

I walk on through a dark, wide corridor in the direction of the canteen. After a while I realize that I must have missed the passage in the wall which leads to the exit. On my way back it catches my eye immediately, and I wonder how I could have overlooked it.

Now I am outside running and cover ground so lightly and easily that it feels like flying.

The foundling

I have discovered a baby in a baby car seat under a low metal structure like a covered bike stand. A passer-by, a woman, stops to watch me kneeling down beside the baby and talking to it. I turn to her suggesting that we should fill in a form as a message for passers-by or the baby´s relatives and leave it with the baby. Now, an official arrives. Still kneeling beside the baby, I tell her what we want to do, and she is listening.

When I finally stand up, one of my ear plugs rolls under the metal structure. The roof is so low, now, that I shy away from crawling under it. For a little while I stand looking at the spot where it disappeared, then turn away regretfully.

The question   July 16

At a work party. On my way to the stage I walk by a table occupied by older male colleagues. Mr A asks me in a booming voice:

'And what do you spray your plants with?'

I don't use any chemicals, flashes through my mind, but I hold myself back, because I know from my parents' experience about the diseases that can befall a fruit tree. Anyway, the truly honest answer would be: I don't have a garden. That's why I don't know what I would do. As this implies that I don't own a house, contrary to most of my older colleagues, I pretend not to have heard the question and walk on.

Change   July 20

My mobile is ringing. I grab for it hastily. The photo of C with her partner flashes on the screen, happy faces, head leaning against head.

'Hello C,' I say.

After a short break she erupts, furious.

'When will you start accepting me as I am?' she fumes.

What on earth does she mean? I wonder quite shaken. Only then do I recollect that she wants to be called Olive, now. Apparently, I have taken this too lightly. She seems to be very serious about it.

'Sorry,' I sigh cursing myself and hoping that the tone of my voice conveys my painful regrets.

Though I have been gazing at the profile photo all the time, it hasn´t occurred to me until this moment that she must have dyed her hair. It is flaming red. And does she wear it short, now? I ask myself. No, it´s still long at the back, but layered around her face. Unfamiliar, but beautiful nevertheless. She is still speaking, in a calmer voice though, and I notice that it is deeper than I remember it to be.[13]

No detour

It is the last leg of a walk in the mountains. J and I are about to climb downhill. We make headway easily and walk so fast that I struggle to take in the surroundings. The rock formations on the ground remind me that on a hill nearby there are sculptures from the Stone Age, which I have looked at recently. Absolutely worth seeing. Yet, J does not want to make the detour. I feel a touch of disappointment but refrain from trying to persuade her otherwise. So we continue on our way downhill.[14]

---

[13] The context is the video *Salt Coast, Foul Wind* with the former Kate Tempest performing as Kae Tempest.
[14] The likely point of reference are the mammoth bone sculptures carved by cave dwellers on the Swabian Alb

The model railway

I have reached the head of the staircase in W´s house and stand looking around the converted attic. A large model railway is laid out all over the floor. On closer examination there are two vast loops separated from each other by a landscape. Other than expected, it is impossible to sit down and make oneself comfortable anywhere, there.

The plant   July 30

In the centre of the converted attic, which is my room, the branches of a palm-like plant stretch towards the frame under the roof. Its foliage nestles in the hollows between the beams. I remember bringing it home from school, when it was little. Could I be suspected of stealing it? The thought makes me feel uncomfortable. It has gained so much in height and volume that it fits perfectly into this space, now. It would be as good as impossible to carry it out unharmed

---

about 40000 years ago. Some of them are exhibited in museums in Blaubeuren, Tübingen and Ulm in Germany.

Danger

There are two camps on the mountainside. I hang around in the one uphill with T, a younger man. A party is going to take place later. We are given the task to take the car and fetch ready-to-eat dishes for a buffet from the camp downhill.

On our arrival I use the opportunity to change into a pair of trousers and a sweat shirt, because now that it is evening it is getting chillier, fast. Suddenly there is an air raid alert, not the sound of a siren but red lights flashing. A humming makes me look up, and I see a drone approaching the camp. It is hard to believe.

A car pulls up. A man leans out of the window and starts a conversation with T about a study he published. T says that he agrees with it, because it is made of …. – he struggles for words – recycled paper, sustainable. In spite of the friendly tone of the exchange there is a looming threat. I am afraid that the man is going to detain T.

Left behind   August 3

H and I are staying with a family in a village in a deep valley of the Black Forest surrounded by steep hillsides. There is no snow. It is dark outside with bulging clouds hanging low. Not unusual for winter.

H is offered a ride to the ski area, but there is no space for me in the car. I am eager to go skiing, too, and I look out of the window longingly, thinking about how to get there on my own. I'll check if there is a bus to Falkau with a stop in our village.

The tick   August 5

It is summer. I sit on one step of a staircase somewhere outdoors. Looking for an itch on the skin of my underbelly, I discover a black spot on a fold, there. It is a huge tick, swollen with my blood. I am aware that I have to remove it expertly. Hopefully, the blood won't spray all over the place, when I apply my pair of pincers.

Cashing up

I count out money on the work surface of our staff kitchen. While our vice head teacher is watching, I pile up stacks of twenty cent coins, then stacks of five cent coins until it adds up to the required total. When I have finished, he nods his approval in his characteristically dignified manner.

An accident   August 15

I am in the kitchen of my parents´ house when I hear a bang and then the crashing and crunching of folding sheet metal from outside. I look out of the window and my heart contracts painfully, because my father is kneeling in the street on all fours with his face contorted with pain. I fear for his life.

Crocodiles   August 21

I am standing on a bridge overlooking a river. Suddenly I notice the scaled body tapering towards the tail and then the enormous head with hooded eyes and with the long snout closing around two rows of pointed teeth of an enormous crocodile lying alongside the left river bank. It is unbelievable, but now, I remember having heard about it. It is supposed to be harmless, though. Really?

At once, I spot more members of the species lining up behind the crocodile, similarly huge, with big scales of different shapes, like armour plate on the one, on the other like rings of sheet iron. They are docked on shore like boats. So I assume that they are safe, which is reassuring because C is down there, nearby.

Regardless, the first crocodile slides onto the river bank. I call out, warning her not to run by any means and admire her, when she starts to move slowly sideward beyond the animal´s angle of vision. When she speeds up, however, I fear that the crocodile is going to chase her. Luckily, she seems to have escaped. What a relief!

The book shelf   August 23, 2022

I am in a children´s bedroom looking at the books in a tall shelf which covers the whole of one wall. Some of them seem familiar. They are classics of youth literature and novels for young adults. Then, there are also multi-volume series and large picture books about countries and about art.

'You have already got a real library,' I say to the teenage girl, who is standing beside me, and advise her to borrow books from the town library from time to time. This way she can find out if she likes an author or if a series is worth pursuing after the first volume.

On a farm

I ride my bike into a farm yard and offer my help to the young farmer who is working in the yard. He replies that there is nothing to do. Perhaps the back-breaking harvest time is already behind them, I conclude.

But now something is about to happen. People are gathering around the farmer and his wife in front of one of the farm buildings. He starts to read out from a slim volume as if it was a holy text. At first I wonder if it can be my book *Nevertheless be Free* but it is slimmer and has a different cover. The author is his daughter. In my footsteps, flashes through my mind.

Epilogue

Why stop at this point? In sixteen months, I have transcribed 137 dreams. As this prime number indicates, the final full stop has been set somewhat arbitrarily. Yet, in their variety my dream narratives can provide glances at the workings of a human consciousness. They set out from different everyday situations, deal with relationships to people in various roles and deal with central human experiences. While proof reading I sometimes caught myself smiling. I would be honoured, if this happened to my readers, too.